Mission Baby Tooth

(Book 2)

Carol Bates Hutchinson

Copyright © 2024 by Carol Bates Hutchinson

All rights reserved. This book or any of its portion may not be reproduced or transmitted in any means, electronic or mechanical, including recording, photocopying, or by any information storage and retrieval system, without the prior written permission of the copyright holder except in the case of brief quotations embodied in critical reviews and other noncommercial uses permitted by copyright law.

Printed in the United States of America
Library of Congress Control Number: 2024920318
ISBN: Softcover   979-8-89518-342-7
        e-Book   979-8-89518-343-4
Published by: WP Lighthouse
Publication Date: 09/20/2024

To buy a copy of this book, please contact:
WP Lighthouse
Phone: +1-888-668-2459
support@wplighthouse.com
wplighthouse.com

Dedicated to those who believe in the magic of fairytales
and
to all the children who give us the reason to write them

MISSION BABY TOOTH

There's a lot of excitement in Tooth Fairy Town,
the race to be won and the teeth to be found.

The tooth fairy tots are getting prepared,
for a celebration beyond compare.

A magnificent feast to welcome them home,
decorations all over wherever you roam.

The baker has a big pie in the oven.
He's mixing up cookies and cakes by the dozen.

The plates and the silver on the table so nice,
such a perfect display, oh what a delight!

The chairs are all polished, the room all in place,
the table all trimmed with pink ribbons and lace.

It won't be too long, they'll be home very soon,
everyone is invited, there's still lots of room!

Who will be first to cross over the line,
with the most teeth and be back on time?

The trophy is sitting on the table so bright,
to be claimed by the winner on this very night.

TOOTH FAIRY TROUBLE

The tooth fairies are busy on earth you can see,
their packs are all full of those baby teeth.

Robbie can hardly hold on to his pack,
he has to prepare for the flight to go back.

To Tooth Fairy Town, he hardly can wait,
to find out if he has won this great race.

He is ready to fly to Tooth Fairy Town,
his pack is so full he can barely leave ground.

The flight will be hard and will take a long time,
to finish and win and cross over that line.

He's now on his way, when he looks to the right,
Tooth Fairy Lil has yet to take flight.

He sees trouble and wonders why Lil is behind,
for he knows he will lose if he's not on time.

To help his friend Lil, he has to go back.
What could be wrong with Lil and her pack?

Lil is trying so hard to fly,
her wing is all broken and torn on the side.

She needs lots of help and is happy to see,
that Robbie has come to her aid, thankfully!

The hope of him winning this race is all gone,
but his friendship with Lil will always be strong.

He helps mend her wing to take the flight back,
to Tooth Fairy Town, they'll surely get back.

In time for the party and celebration to see,
Who won this great race to collect the most teeth?

TRUE FRIEND

The tooth fairies all get in a long line,
to have the teeth counted and weighed at this time.

Each pack is so full they hardly know how,
the tooth fairies got back to Tooth Fairy Town.

The Tooth Fairy Queen will announce who won,
she'll be counting the teeth from dusk until dawn.

She needs lots of help from the tooth fairy tots,
to count every tooth and never to stop.

The time has come, an announcement is made,
the winner declared, what a wonderful day!

For the winner is Tommy and he stands very proud,
as she hands him the trophy in front of the crowd.

They all stand and cheer as Tommy stands tall,
the fastest, the strongest, the bravest of all.

The Tooth Fairy Queen is so proud to say,
there's someone else who deserves an award this day.

Robbie at the table and sitting so proud,
the Tooth Fairy Queen is speaking so loud.

"Robbie you are a true friend indeed,
to Tooth Fairy Lil who was in such great need."

"You came to her aid when she needed you most,
the kindness you've shown, I am ready to boast."

"This ribbon I give you to be worn all the time,
a reminder to all for you being so kind."

Robbie was happy and very proud,
Lil smiled and stood up in front of the crowd.

Hurrah to Robbie, everyone cheered!
and Robbie was grinning from ear to ear.

THE GREAT ANNOUNCEMENT

The celebration went on till the end of the day,
such a grand time for all when an announcement was made.

The time has come in Tooth Fairy Town,
to build the new school, they need to break ground.

The baby teeth gathered from the great race,
will be the beginning of much work to take place.

The plans have been made for the walls and the stairs,
the flag pole in front will show the way there.

How exciting to build such a wonderful school,
a place where you learn and all teachers will rule.

The playground, gymnasium, and the field to the right,
we'll be working all day and well into the night.

Everyone works, no one is spared,
so many baby teeth, all handled with care.

Stacking and packing, the walls are soon up,
the cupboards and book shelves will all soon be stuffed.

To build a new school is such a great task,
and a job never ending, and no time for naps!

When this work is all done and the school is complete,
each tooth fairy tot will then take their seat.

And be proud of the school that was built just for them,
a place to learn lessons while making new friends.

DOGS TO WALK!

The tooth fairy tots are now on their way,
to walk all the dogs that need walking today.

To the pet shop they go and what do they find?
The dogs are all standing and waiting in line.

The dogs are all anxious, they all want to walk!
but they must wait their turn if they like it or not.

The first dog to walk is a shaggy short tail,
he heads for the corner at Baby Tooth Trail.

The walk is a mile and up a steep mountain,
all dogs get a treat and a drink from the fountain.

The tooth fairy tots know they have to get back,
there are more dogs to walk, so they must stay on track.

Next in line is a huge dog, his name is Big Moe,
he is stubborn and awkward and walks rather slow.

He looks quite ferocious, but he's rather sweet,
when he barks you can hear him clear down to Main Street.

Every tooth fairy knows that dog named Big Moe,
if he sits very long, he might have to be towed!

THE TRAIN TO TOOTH MOUNTAIN

The train to Tooth Mountain is on its way,
it leaves from the station on this very day.

Each car is in place and ready to go,
the train takes off at a speed rather slow.

It's all full of baby teeth and going down the track,
headed for Tooth Mountain to unload and unpack.

A magnificent tower to be built and tall as can be,
a place to look out and as far as you see.

You'll look over the valley and over the town,
such a beautiful view when you look down.

The steps to the top will be hard to climb,
but the tooth fairies will have the option to fly.

But not all tooth fairies like to fly,
for they love to walk and get exercise.

So some walk the steps and others may fly,
but how they will choose, we will never know why.

THE QUEENS' CROWN

The Tooth Fairy Queen, she needs a new crown,
the one that she has is so old and worn down.

She has asked all the tooth fairies to think of a way,
to design a new crown for her head to display.

A contest will take place in Tooth Fairy Town,
to decide and to make the Queens' tooth fairy crown.

For the Tooth Fairy Queen has instructions we've found,
to find all the gems that are all under ground.

To Miracle Street with a shovel in hand,
to look for the treasures and dig up the land.

Beautiful gems and crystals will shine,
will glitter and glow, what a grand design!

The Queen will be pleased and so very proud,
that her head will be Oh so perfectly crowned!

Who will win such a contest, who will win the design?
The Tooth Fairy Queen will finally decide!

When the contest is won and a decision is made,
the Tooth Fairy Queen will stop and she'll say,

"A new challenge for all, your toughest one yet,
will take lots of skill for this mysterious quest!"

"So go now, get ready and pack all your things,
Who knows what this mystery and great journey will bring!"

Carol Bates Hutchinson

"Where does the tooth go Mom?"

This was the simple question her children would ask that would inspire a story and years later would evolve into a new and imaginative fairytale.

With a love for creative writing, Carol has created a delightful book series of a magical kingdom known as Tooth Fairy Town and the many adventures of the tooth fairies who inhabit this enchanted village. Carol enjoys the art of lyrical writing and weaving words together to create a sweet story line of imaginative tales. Carol resides in Ohio. In her free time, she loves and enjoys spending time with her family and friends, traveling new sites and visiting scenic locations, especially those with mountains. She has worked as a medical secretary and volunteered at the schools her children attended. With her writing, Carol hopes to capture the magic of childhood and keep it alive. She believes in cherishing that childlike wonder that can often get lost in today's fast-paced world. Her stories aim to inspire readers to hold onto that magic today and for many future years to come.

www.ingramcontent.com/pod-product-compliance
Lightning Source LLC
LaVergne TN
LVHW070741060225
802923LV00002B/22